Ginger Josie in WARTIME

by

Ann Flint

Grosvenor House
Publishing Limited

This book is published by
Grosvenor House Publishing Ltd
28-30 High Street, Guildford, Surrey, GU1 3EL.
www.grosvenorhousepublishing.co.uk

A CIP record for this book
is available from the British Library

ISBN 978-1-78148-459-3

For Michael, my husband,
who also lived through World War Two
as an evacuee in Wales.

Thanks to Helen Barker,
who types my stories for me
and manages to read my writing.

Chapter 1

Josie Jenkins was born four years before the war began. Four years of peace and quiet, which Josie couldn't really remember. Mum said there wasn't much peace and quiet anyway when Josie was around.

Years before anyone called her 'Ginger', Josie had golden curls; at least that's what Mum told her. People said she was a beautiful baby, but with a terrible temper. When the gold turned to ginger, everyone blamed her temper on her 'red' hair. When crossed, Josie would hold her breath until she turned blue and her mum was afraid she was going to die. It was even worse when she did it behind a closed door – *that* really scared them!

Josie lived in a newly built semi-detached house on the edge of a village. The house had a large garden which Dad had made and at the end of the lawn were two baby apple trees, one of eating apples and one of cooking apples. Dad also had raspberry canes, black and redcurrants, a pear tree and rhubarb. He also grew salad items and vegetables. The hedges were made of privet, but only little baby plants so Josie could very easily see over, which also made it easy to make friends with the neighbours. Mr and Mrs Crane lived on one side and Josie spent so much time there that Dad made a gate in the hedge opposite the back door for 'popping in'. Mrs Crane was much older than Mum and had a 'big boy', who was almost grown up. Mrs Crane had always wanted a little girl and she loved to 'borrow' Josie. Josie in turn liked being borrowed, though she wasn't too keen on the big boy, who hardly ever spoke to her. Mrs Crane became her beloved godmother.

As it was a new estate with lots of young families, there were many children to play with. Josie's best friend was David. David was born one month before Josie and their mothers were friends so Josie and David lay together on a blanket, kicking each other, before they could even walk and talk. Because David was one month older and a boy, he always thought he was the boss, but Josie knew better.

Opposite David's house and a few doors down from Josie's were the Price boys; with only nineteen months between them, they often played together, but they also played with Josie and David.

Mr and Mrs Smart lived higher up the street with their children, Shirley and Tony. They lived in a larger detached house, with a swing in the garden. Josie was a frequent visitor, not only for the swing but also for the generously given glasses of 'pop'.

At the very top of the street, right on the corner, was the home of Elizabeth, who was a couple of years older than Josie. Elizabeth was everything Josie aspired to be; she was clever and pretty and good at most things. She enjoyed friendship with Josie in spite of the age difference and, if Josie wasn't with David or swinging or drinking pop at the Smarts', she was with Elizabeth at her house.

Before the builders stopped building because of the war, they built a street of houses behind Josie's house. Because Josie's garden was so long and so was the new house, they didn't see the new neighbours very often. The Proctors, as they were called, had a boy named Brian and a girl named Nina. Sometimes Dad would chat over the back hedge to Mr and Mrs Proctor (who also liked gardening). Josie would stand with Dad to gossip and talked to Nina. She liked Nina and, had they lived in the same street, they would have been good friends.

Lastly there was Margaret-Rose, who lived at the bottom of the street in a house built later than Josie's and almost on the Common. Margaret-Rose was older than Josie, but she had a younger brother called Douglas who was Josie's age, who also played with Josie and the boys.

The road that made the top bar of a T across Josie's road had lots of girls living on it. They were what Josie called 'sissies' because they played ball and whip and top and skipping and kept their hair tidy and their dresses clean. Josie was useless with a ball and couldn't skip, so when they called for her she would make herself scarce, knowing that they only wanted her to turn the end of the rope not tied to a lamppost, or to be the pig forever in the middle.

One day when Joan, Betty and her cohorts were playing a half decent game outside Josie's house, Josie tried to join in. Joan folded her arms and announced, 'Mummy says I haven't to play with you anymore because you're too rough.' Josie's mother took offence at this criticism of her daughter and the girls from Vernon Road were 'discouraged' from playing in Josie's street.

A favourite visitor to the street was the Bread Man. He had a pony and trap and Josie adored his pony. One day, when Josie met him outside, he asked her if she would like a ride on the trap. Of course Josie answered with a breathless, 'Yes!' She was instructed to go and ask her mother's permission whilst he delivered bread to a neighbour. Josie couldn't be bothered to ask Mum; anyway, she might say no, you could never tell with grown-ups.

An hour or so later all the neighbours were out looking for her as Josie proudly trotted the pony back, holding the reins herself, to a real scolding not only from Mum, but from everybody who had been searching.

Another thing that made Mum cross was Josie's habit of running about all summer long without any shoes on her feet. Mum said it made it look as if she was too poor to afford shoes, but Josie liked the feel of all the different surfaces beneath her bare feet. Then, of course, there was the problem of where the discarded shoes had been left!

War was declared on 3 September 1939. That September was Josie's first day at school. She had been looking forward to going to school for ages. Josie's best friend David started school on the same day. All the grown-ups were fussing about was the war, but Josie and David were only interested in finding out what school was like.

'I don't like school,' Josie said after a week. 'I don't think I'll go anymore.'

David didn't mind it as much. 'You have to go until you're grown up,' he said. Josie was horrified. Everything was so boring.

One day when Josie had made every picture possible with the picture blocks, she asked for something else to do. 'You can't have done *all* of them, do them again,' said Miss Andrews.

Then Josie discovered that the paper on a little corner of a block was coming loose. She picked at it. She picked again and again until the picture on that side of the block was gone and it lay in shreds on her table. This was much more interesting. Josie tried another corner, then another, until the picture block was completely bereft of its pictures. Suddenly Josie was aware of someone behind her. 'What do you think you are doing, Josie Jenkins?' asked Miss Andrews grimly. Josie didn't have an answer. 'Go to the Headteacher's room.'

'No,' said Josie defiantly.

'Then I'll take you,' Miss Andrews said and, taking Josie by the scruff of her neck, began to march her towards the door. Josie screamed loudly. In fact she screamed all the way to the Head's room, lying down so she had to be dragged all through the connecting classrooms. The rest of the school watched with interest, it certainly livened things up, and on that day Josie got her reputation as 'that naughty little ginger girl from the babies' class'.

Josie spent a long time in the Head's room and emerged a sadder and wiser girl.

Josie's next cause for complaint was music, which she actually loved, but every week she put up her hand for a drum and was ignored. Josie asked politely, 'Please may I have a drum?'

'No dear,' replied Miss Andrews. 'The drums are for the boys. You little girls can have the tambourines and the triangles.'

'But I want a turn on the drum,' shouted Josie, 'I'm not playing a sissy triangle again,' and she flung the offending triangle on the floor.

'Go to the Head's office,' said the teacher again and this time Josie went quietly. She knew the way by now, and was to know it more and more as the first year progressed.

A huge air raid shelter appeared in the playground. No air raids had happened yet, but the children had to prepare in case there were any. When the siren went, Josie had to leave everything straightaway and line up at the classroom door to march to the shelter. There was no room to do anything but sit in the air raid shelter because the whole infants' school was in there. Josie found it much more interesting than lessons. They sang, chanted tables, recited poems, plus any other entertainment that could be thought of. Then the 'all clear' siren went and they all marched back to class again.

Josie and all the other children were issued with gas masks, which had to be carried (in a square cardboard box) over the shoulder at all times. Josie's class, mostly under-fives, were given Mickey Mouse gas masks and Josie soon discovered that you could use your gas mask to make rude noises through the rubber and instructed everyone else how to do it. This did not go down very well with the teachers.

Because Josie's dad looked after their garden so well and was so proud of it, she was surprised one weekend when he and the neighbours from either side were digging a big hole in the vegetable patch. 'What are they all doing?' asked Josie.

'Digging a hole for the Anderson shelter,' said Mum.

'What's an Anderson shelter?' Josie was puzzled.

'It's for when they start bombing us, to keep us safe,' Mum replied. 'The Government are sending them and we have to half-bury them in the garden. It will be made of corrugated iron – you know, that wavy metal stuff that they put on shed roofs.'

When it came, it was bedded in and Dad put earth and rocks and flowers and made a rockery over it to cover it up so it didn't look too bad, but Josie hated it. The air raid siren would go in the middle of the night and they all had to get up and go down the garden and into the shelter. It was cold and scary.

The first time the siren went, Dad carried Josie to the shelter but Mum never appeared. Dad went back and met her halfway down the garden path, half dressed. 'What were you doing?' asked Dad crossly as he and Mum entered the shelter.

'Getting dressed,' was the reply. Mum whispered, 'I couldn't find my knickers so I haven't got any on.'

'You don't get dressed when the siren goes, you put on your coat and shoes and come straight out!' shouted Dad. 'If a bomb drops on the house, it won't matter what you're wearing.'

In the dark, Josie could hear Mum sniffing. She was obviously upset, so Josie snuggled up to her and gave her a cuddle.

Josie's favourite grown-up (after her Mum and Dad, of course) was Grandma. She only had one grandma and she was very special. If Josie had been in trouble at home or at school, as was often the case, she would run on ahead of her parents to get to Gran's first so she could give her version of events, and Grandma would always be on Josie's side.

Josie's family always went to visit Grandma on a Sunday and most times stayed for tea. That September an order for 'blackout' was made. This meant that there were no street lights. As the nights drew in and it got dark earlier and earlier, it became difficult walking back from Grandma's. Mum, Dad and Josie each had a torch, but they were only allowed to point it down to the ground. White stripes were painted on the roads and lampposts to help.

There were no traffic lights either and there were lots of accidents. Mum told Josie that lots of people had been killed in road accidents. It was very frightening. Dads were told to walk with white shirt tails hanging out at the back so they could be followed. People were told to walk facing the traffic in pavementless country lanes, which made it doubly scary.

Mum had to make curtains of black material and hang them as a lining to all their normal curtains to make sure no chink of light escaped. An ARP (Air Raid Precautions) warden would come round to check and shout at them if he could see any light. Josie was not a coward, but the blackness in her bedroom was so total that she imagined all sorts of things were in there with her.

Josie already wished that the war was over!

Chapter 2

Every day Josie had to walk to school with Mum, walk home and back for lunch, and home again at the end of school. It was quite a long walk four times a day but, as there were no school dinners or packed lunches, it had to be done.

When mums began war work and dads were away fighting the war, school dinners began, but only children of parents who were war working were allowed to have them. Josie wasn't eligible but, according to what the other children told her, she didn't think she was missing much!

One day Josie arrived home for lunch to a strange-looking pie. Josie was suspicious. 'What have you put in it?' she asked.

'Potatoes and meat,' replied Mum with a sigh.

'Why have you put potatoes *in* the pie and *with* the pie?' asked Josie.

'It's because I don't have enough meat. It's rationing.'

'What's that?' queried Josie, puzzled.

'It's to share everything out. Meat is rationed and we have to make it go further.' Josie didn't think much of that idea.

Next time they went shopping, Mum did something else she had never done before. She bought one of the poor dead furry rabbits that were hanging up outside the butcher's shop. Josie hated seeing these and the dead chickens and pheasants, still in their feathers, so she went to the next door shop to look at the fruit and vegetables at the greengrocer's.

Mum took the dead rabbit out of her basket at home. Josie felt so sad for it. Then, with one swift movement, Mum ripped the skin off the rabbit, leaving it naked and pink. It made a horrible tearing noise when Mum skinned the rabbit and Josie screamed.

'You'll have to get used to it from now on,' Mum said grimly and made rabbit stew.

Just after Josie had begun school in September, the Government held a National Registration Day. Everyone had to give in their name, address, birth date, age, etc. Later they used all the details to give everyone, even Josie, an identity card, which said who she was and had to be carried at all times, and a ration book. Josie's was green because she was a child. Mum and Dad had a different colour. They had a pale fawn colour. Inside were a lot of coupons. The coupons had to be given in with the money when something was paid for. When the coupons for that week were used up, you couldn't have anything else, even if you had the money. To begin with it was only for meat, later it was for everything – even sweets. Josie had been used to popping into one of the little shops which were on every corner on the way home from school and having a little paper cone of dolly mixtures or jelly babies, which cost a farthing (a quarter of a penny). Now she could only do that once a week. She also had to get used to dried eggs in a tin, dried milk for cooking and rubbery cheese.

One day there was a knock at the door. Mum answered it to a lady holding a sheaf of papers. 'Could you take an evacuee?' asked the lady.

'Oh, yes! Please, Mum, can we have one?' Josie had heard about evacuees. They were children who had been sent out of the cities likely to be bombed. So far Josie had not even heard a bomb.

Mum reluctantly said yes and Josie was very excited. 'Will it be a boy or a girl? How old will it be?'

'I don't know,' said the lady. 'I'll let you know details later.'

13

Sadly Josie never got her evacuee because it was decided that Josie's village was under a bombing route to and from the big cities, where they made guns (munitions they called them), also tanks and bombs and they were at risk themselves.

Josie was having trouble learning to read, mostly because she never listened or concentrated. Her mother was sent for and asked if she would hear her read every single day. Reluctantly Josie read to her mum.

'Why can't you remember the words?' said Mum, exasperated.

'There are too many,' said Josie.

'Well, you don't have to learn every word in the world,' said Mum.

'I don't?' said Josie, surprised.

'No. If you know the letter sounds, you can build up the words yourself.'

'Even hard ones?'

'Sometimes. Now, let's start again. I'll make sure you know what the letter sounds are and we'll try some different books.'

Mum was right! It was like a miracle; once Josie twigged it, she could read like magic. She read everything in sight. Luckily Elizabeth had lots of books from before the war and was happy to lend them. Before long even they were finished and Mum decided Josie would join the library in the town. It was a bus ride away and Mum had to take her. She was only allowed one book at a time. In the library, Josie stood amazed. She couldn't believe that there were so many books in the world. She also began to get *Sunny Stories* by Enid Blyton. It came out every week as a little booklet, a bit like a comic.

Even the elderly neighbours lent books. Really old-fashioned books, leather covered and embossed in gold with their titles, the pages gold edged. The few pictures were called 'plates' and were covered with tissue. The books were to be treated reverently, but good stories nevertheless.

Her youngest auntie had a set of *Children's Encyclopaedias* by Arthur Mee. Josie was often to be found deep in them when she visited Granny's house.

Josie wanted her own books. She loved the feel and smell of them, but paper was scarce. Newspapers had shrunk in size and fewer books were being published, making them more expensive, but the main reason that Josie's parents didn't buy her books was because she read so quickly. They said it wasn't worth it. She still got her *Rupert Annual* at Christmas, and read and reread it until the next one arrived.

Then Great Uncle Harry from London came to stay. He was the most exciting person imaginable. He was 'high up' in the Post Office in London and called Josie his 'petite chérie', which Josie thought was 'petty sherry'. Josie knew it was French because Great Uncle Harry had told her and being called it felt very exotic. Best of all, Great Uncle Harry had come armed with paper! He had lined foolscap books that were no longer in use. He had pulled out all the used bits, but there was still lots of paper for Josie to write and draw on.

From being an avid reader, Josie now also became an avid writer. She wrote her own stories and illustrated them. Great Uncle Harry couldn't have bought her anything better. He had lots of exciting stories to tell her and Josie was really sorry when he had to go back to London again.

A week later a parcel arrived, the first parcel that had ever arrived addressed just to her. Inside was a book, a new one; inside the book was a message: 'To the bookworm, ma petite chérie, Josie.' How Josie loved Great Uncle Harry for understanding.

Another source of paper in these days of paper shortage was the local printer. He stapled together offcuts (from printing jobs) in plain and coloured paper to make little books, charging a penny or a halfpenny. Josie filled them with stories in tiny writing and illustrated by her own little pictures.

Next door to the printer's was the Co-op. Mum went in every week because the ration books were registered with them. Josie sat on the counter and sang 'You are my sunshine, my only sunshine' when she was younger and was rewarded with broken biscuits from the bottom of the glass-fronted display boxes.

Next to reading and writing, Josie liked art. She enjoyed painting so much that she never wanted the lesson to end, so when it came to lining up at the door, she was always at the back. This didn't bother Josie but one day there was so much pushing and shoving in the line that Josie fell over.

'Miss, she's spilt the paint!' Someone couldn't wait to tell tales.

Then someone else said, 'It's not paint; it's blood.' This brought the teacher hurrying over.

It was indeed blood. Josie had hit her head on the iron feet of the double desks. This was very interesting, so Josie didn't cry. Her mother was sent for and had to take Josie out of school to go and have her head stitched. A big bandage covered the wound, which pleased Josie enormously because she felt very important, also they went to one of the new Civic Restaurants because she had missed her dinner. It was the first time Josie had ever eaten a meal out and the restaurant greatly impressed her. So much so that she began to play 'restaurants', making food out of plasticine on doll's tea-set plates. In the summer the plasticine was replaced by berries and leaves.

Every Saturday morning, Josie went to dancing class. Mum took her on the bus into town. Madame Rollison's studio was above a row of shops and was reached by walking through a confectioner's shop. This was the best bit for Josie because the shop sold one-penny chocolate wafer biscuits without a coupon. Josie was allowed one every Saturday. Josie also got to wear a ballet tutu. It was made out of Mum's wedding dress and had white frills and little rosebuds over the skirt, and Josie got to feel like a real ballerina wearing it.

The third best thing about dancing class was that the children were part of the local Panto. Josie enjoyed performing even though she wasn't a very good dancer. This year they were putting on *Dick Whittington*. One of the scenes that the children were dancing in was the scene where Dick sets sail to make his fortune. The dancers had to do a sailors' hornpipe. It was tricky to remember all the steps, but Josie managed it, except for one evening when there was a disaster. It was Josie's navy sailor skirt. She was just doing the 'climbing the rigging' actions – hand over hand as if she was climbing a rope – when the elastic in her skirt began to slip. Josie didn't know if she should climb the rigging or hold the skirt up. She chose the rigging and the skirt began to slide down – and the audience began to laugh. Then the skirt fell to her knees and the audience cheered. Then it fell to the ground to a round of applause and she finished the dance in her navy blue school knickers. All the other girls were horrified at the embarrassment of it all, but Josie didn't mind. She liked the sound of the audience laughing and the round of applause and knew that she enjoyed making people laugh.

Chapter 3

Josie's grandad used to tap dance all the way down the stairs. He was Dad's dad and great fun. He had six sons and Josie's dad was the eldest. They didn't have a mother because she had died of pneumonia when Dad was a boy. They had been brought up by a succession of housekeepers. None of the housekeepers lasted very long. They were driven out by the boys' arguments and the tricks played.

It came as a great shock to Josie when she heard that Grandad was very ill and had asked to see her and her cousin Angela, who was eleven months younger.

The girls went fearfully into a darkened room full of people. Grandad didn't look like his jolly self. He didn't know who was Josie or who was Angela and kept getting them mixed and spoke in a peculiar way. Josie and Angela couldn't wait to get out. Once outside, Josie burst into tears. 'I want proper

Grandad back,' she cried. It was no surprise next day to be told that Grandad had died. No more tap dancing lessons from the grandad who could tap his way down the stairs!

Grandad's death meant that Dad's youngest brother was without a home and someone had to look after him, even though Josie thought Henry was nearly grown up and could look after himself. He came to live at Josie's house. Josie didn't mind because he was rarely there. He was an apprentice at Grandad's works and out there all day. (Grandad had made all his sons start at the bottom!) Henry was out most evenings too. He smelt of tobacco and drink when he did come home. Josie could hear him being told off as she lay in bed. She felt sorry for him because he was an orphan and probably missing his dad.

Most children at school didn't have dads at home anymore. The dads had been 'called up' to serve in the war. Josie was lucky because her dad was in a 'reserved occupation' and was needed to stay at home and run things in England. Dad was a fire warden though and an aircraft spotter. He was often out during the night on duty and still had to go to work next day. He had a notebook full of drawings of aircraft so he could tell whose side they were on. Dad caught Josie reading it one day and told her off.

It was a good job that Dad did come home in the middle of the night. Josie, Mum and Henry were asleep upstairs and Dad could smell burning. He checked the kitchen, the dining room and then opened the door to the front room. To his horror, flames surged towards him, so he shut the door again fast. There was obviously a fire raging now that must have been raging for some time. He ran upstairs and roused Mum and Henry and, picking up a sleeping Josie, wrapped her in an eiderdown and carried her downstairs. The hall was filled with smoke and tiny tongues of flame were licking round the front room door. 'There's a fire,' Dad said briefly.

'I want to see,' said Josie. To her dismay Dad carried her out of the house and next door to Mrs Crane's house, where he rang for the Fire Brigade. Mrs Crane put her to bed in a room overlooking the back garden, where she couldn't see anything and missed all the excitement.

Next morning when she looked out of a front window it was horrifying. On the front lawn there was a blackened suite, sideboard and piano. The lead in the leaded lights had melted, so the front room windows had gone, and the room was almost totally black. Josie cried when she thought how close they had all come to dying.

The culprit, thought to have started the fire, was suspected to be Henry. Dad thought Henry must have come in, sat in the armchair, lit a cigarette and fallen asleep. The cigarette must have fallen down the side of the armchair and smouldered for ages, while he went upstairs to bed, totally unaware.

'That's it!' said Mum. 'I'm not having him back. Someone else can have a turn; he's got other brothers besides you, Bill.' So Henry went.

Mum's youngest sister joined the Wrens, the Women's Royal Naval Service, and came to say goodbye to Josie when she was out in the street playing with friends. Josie felt very proud of her young auntie in her Wrens uniform with a lovely sailor hat to finish it off.

One of Dad's other brothers, James, joined the Army as a motorcycle dispatch rider. He had to leave his baby son and a girl toddler behind. He was sent abroad.

One day David's mum came to collect David and Josie for lunch, even though it wasn't her turn. All the family were at Josie's house, crying because James had been killed. Josie was very sad too, but not so sad that she didn't tell everyone about her heroic 'Uncle James', who had been killed by Hitler personally, dying bravely in the cause of freedom!

One of the disadvantages of being at a church school was that the children frequently had to go to church. Josie didn't mind so much when she was missing 'sums'. She saw some of her cousins and older friends in the Juniors and couldn't resist waving to them, in spite of being told not to in a teacher's lecture before they walked down the road to the church.

It was funny that the air raid siren never went off when they were in church. Josie thought it was because God wouldn't let Hitler bomb them when they were in there. Josie had great belief in the power of God because her mother did. When Josie asked her mum why there was a war and who would win, Mum always said we would because God and right were on our side. It gave Josie a warm feeling to know that God had chosen her side to support!

Sunday was a special day. They all went to church on Sunday morning and Josie went into Sunday school. The best thing about Sunday school was that she got a little book to put all her bible sticky stamps in. They had to be licked carefully because too much lick made them fall out and then you wouldn't have enough stamps for the Sunday school outing and the Christmas party.

The other thing about Sunday was not so good. Josie and the other children were not allowed to play; in fact, you couldn't do anything much. Mum was very strict about that. No drawing or painting, no sewing or knitting, and certainly no running about wildly outside. Josie was allowed to read, thank goodness, and she was so pleased that she was now a good reader.

Even though there was a war on, Josie still went to friends' birthday parties and had one herself. All the mums were very clever at making things. Those who had babies and therefore 'clinic baby orange' made orange jelly from that and gelatine bought at the chemist's. They also bought rennet there and made junket, which was a cross between milk jelly and blancmange. Rations were shared between mums to make birthday cake and Josie's mum made brilliant fudge from condensed milk. Josie enjoyed all parties, especially her own of course, but she loved other people's too. She was always the last to leave the table, not because she was greedy, but she liked to try a taste of everything on offer!

Another great treat was when Elizabeth, her older friend, cleared out her toy box. Elizabeth's mum made her completely empty it and sort through just before Christmas and her birthday to make room for her new toys. Elizabeth's parents were a lot better off than Josie's parents and, with Elizabeth being older, she 'grew out of' toys too, all of which Josie coveted. Elizabeth was very generous, but Josie also liked the broken bits of toys that had dropped to the very bottom of the box. Josie would fall on them with cries of delight, only to have her mother say, 'What rubbish have you got there?', though Josie usually managed to hold onto them.

Elizabeth also had a cat called Blackie, a female cat that had kittens at regular intervals. Josie loved cats and was always asking for one. She actually saw Blackie's latest lot of kittens just after they had been born, but the next day Blackie only had one. The others had been drowned in a bucket of water. Elizabeth's mother said they were running out of homes for them, but they had left Blackie with one kitten. Obviously Blackie couldn't count, because she didn't seem to be bothered by the fact that she only had one kitten and was a lovely mother to it. Josie pestered her parents and at last they gave in and the kitten was hers.

Sooty liked being cuddled and was often to be seen dressed up in doll's clothes, being wheeled round as Josie's baby in the doll's pram. She was a sweet tempered cat and would put up with being 'loved' by Josie until she'd had enough, and then would stroll away, her tail in the air.

Most times Sooty was around Josie when she played. One time they were out in the street with friends when a dog came running up. Josie was determined to 'save' Sooty from the dog and picked her up. Sooty had other ideas; she clawed her way out of Josie's arms, up her face to the top of her head and leapt for it, easily outrunning the dog, which set off in hot pursuit. The screaming and barking from the street alerted Josie's mum, who came running out to find Josie covered in blood. All Josie could say was, 'It wasn't Sooty's fault. Don't blame Sooty,' in between sobs. Josie's mum was not too fond of Sooty and Josie was worried that she would use the incident to get rid of the cat. In order to stop Josie crying and get a good look at her face, Mum agreed that Sooty was not to blame. It was Josie's fault for picking the cat up to save it.

Josie's face was a bit of a mess. A long deep scratch ran from her lip to her ear but the rest of the scratches were fairly superficial and her eyes were safe, which was what Mum had been worried about. The cat was safe too and Josie learned that day that a cat can generally look after itself!

Chapter 4

Josie knew nothing about Halloween and Bonfire Night because bonfires and fireworks were banned in the blackout. It was a long stretch from the summer holidays to Christmas. Josie knew all about Christmas. Rationing had made everything to be in short supply but it was still an occasion to look forward to.

The uncles and aunties (of whom there were many) always celebrated Christmas together as a family and everyone took it in turn to provide the party.

In the second year of the war, Christmas Eve was spent at Grandma and Grandad's (Mum's mother and father). Josie was so excited. Dad was excited too and he swung Josie round. 'Put me down!' demanded Josie. Dad gave her a final swing, quite close to the fire in the black leaded range. Josie screamed. Mum and Grandma told Dad off. Grandma warned that Father Christmas probably wouldn't bring Dad any Christmas presents as a punishment. Mum agreed that that would be the likely outcome.

Josie, Mum and Dad made their way home through the black streets. The night was cloudy and no moon or stars could be seen. The blackness was total, even the torches only lit the ground before them.

At last they were home and Josie went to bed, too tired to stay awake. She fell asleep to the sound of crackling brown paper and newspaper downstairs. There was no pretty paper to wrap presents in. It had been banned because of the war and the need to save paper.

Josie woke early and crawled down to the bottom of the bed. There was a satisfactorily filled pillowcase, all lumpy and bumpy. Josie took it back to the top of the bed and fell asleep again, clutching the pillowcase.

When daylight came, Josie took her pillowcase into Mum and Dad's bedroom and climbed in the bed and woke them up. Dad had a large pillowcase too. Josie opened her presents first. She had a crocheted doll with some lovely clothes that Mum had made, some doll's house furniture that Dad had made, a Rupert annual, a toy Post Office, a box of paints, coloured pencils and a colouring book.

Now it was Dad's turn. His presents were wrapped in newspaper. Dad unwrapped them slowly. There were potatoes and pieces of coal. Josie was horrified, poor Dad. He said solemnly, 'Well, Grandma and Mum said Father Christmas wouldn't come because I tipped you upside down in front of the fire.' Josie felt so sorry for Dad and vowed that *she* was never going to do anything naughty in the future (at least not on Christmas Eve).

Of course that was a promise that Josie was incapable of keeping. Trouble seemed to follow her around. Like the time she tried to walk from one end of the bay window to the other – on the outside. A concerned neighbour ran round to tell Mum, who was oblivious downstairs.

Then there was the day she met Grandma when she was out, and had asked for some pennies to make enough to buy a bag of chips. She was in so much trouble for that. 'You'd think I'd killed someone,' Josie complained to David.

Then there was the time Josie found a dead cat in the undergrowth at the side of the road near the vicarage. She took all her friends to see it, observing it harden, soften, get covered with flies and full of maggots before someone told the vicar, who buried it and told her mum.

'What were you thinking of?' asked Mum.

'It was so interesting,' protested Josie. 'I was sad for the cat but it was dead anyway and

I couldn't make it better. I just wanted to see what would happen.'

One evening Josie asked Mum and Dad if Elizabeth could stay the night. She asked in front of Elizabeth and her parents, who had delivered her home after having had tea with them. Mum and Dad said no, not this time, it wasn't convenient. Josie was angry; she knew they wouldn't change their minds, but they were going to suffer anyway for saying no. Josie didn't have red hair for nothing. She lay down on the path and had a full-blown temper tantrum. Her mum and dad were embarrassed and ashamed, so were Elizabeth and her parents, but Josie didn't care – serve them right. Dad picked Josie up, screaming still, opened the back door and put her inside. Josie shut up pretty quickly then, when there was no audience.

That summer, Josie and David were inseparable. If you found one of them, the other was nearby. They were both still interested in nature. David was going to be a naturalist. He and his dad made a collection of insects and butterflies, which his dad gassed in a jar and then put a pin through to display and name them, which Josie didn't like. Josie was going to be a zoologist and work with animals, but she wasn't going to gas them and stick pins in them; she was going to care for them.

Josie and David had wonderful imaginary adventures. A saw horse was a plane or a boat and they went to jungles and deserts in their imaginations until someone would call them in for a meal. David had funny parents. His mum was lovely and called him David. His dad was odd and called him John and pretended Josie didn't exist, so Josie tried to keep out of his way, only going inside their house when he wasn't there.

There was a deep dark wood behind David's house and a gloomy pond, surrounded by so many trees that light never penetrated and the surface of the pond was dark green, which only added to the air of mystery.

There was quite a lot of wildlife in and around the pond. Josie found what she thought were lizards on the edge. She caught them and made a home for them in a glass jar filled with soil in which she buried the lizards. When she told her dad, he said they wouldn't be lizards but newts and they tipped out the jar, only to find that the newts were dead. Josie was so sorry and promised that she wouldn't catch and keep creatures until she had found out what they were and what sort of home they needed.

Josie and David decided they were going to marry and go exploring the world when they grew up. They weren't going to have any children though; they would get in the way when they were exploring the jungle. Josie was a little sad about that, but she thought if she had some baby monkeys, she could train them and they would cuddle her as if she were their mum, so she wouldn't miss not having babies so much.

Chapter 5

The Anderson shelter was used less and less. They all decided they'd rather take shelter under the stairs. When it rained, the shelter could be ankle deep in water and Josie needed her wellingtons on. It was dank and damp and dark in the Anderson shelter. Snails enjoyed it though and sometimes if you sat on one you heard a crunch. One night Mum let out a scream when something cold and wet landed on her lap. It was a frog that had decided that the shelter was an ideal home. 'That does it,' said Mum. 'I'm never going back in that shelter.'

Then a large metal package was delivered. Josie couldn't wait for Dad to get home so she could find out what it was. Dad was most annoying and wouldn't say. It was like a large jigsaw puzzle. Finally all the pieces were together and it looked like a giant cage. 'What is it?' asked Josie.

'It's a Morrison shelter,' said Dad. 'It's made of steel and very strong. We three will sleep in it. If there is an air raid in the night, we will be already in. You'll get in first, Josie, when it's your bedtime. Then Mum and finally I will get into it when it's our bedtime. We can use it as a big table as well.'

Josie looked at it doubtfully. 'It's an awfully big table. Where will we put our legs?' she said.

'We'll just have to manage,' laughed Dad.

The next week they had a chance to try it out as a table when Josie's aunts and cousins came to tea. Josie helped Mum to lay the table. Mum was the eldest in her family; her brothers had children all around Josie's age. Josie had been right, it was difficult to sit round the table, but they managed it with a great deal of hilarity.

It was almost like a party. Mum opened some of her bottled fruit, a big Kilner jar of pears from her own tree which she had bottled last summer. Mum also bottled plums and blackcurrants. She also made jam from the fruit in the garden, so she had made some jam tarts. They had salad, also from the garden, and ham. Josie asked where the ham had come from. She was told not to ask, and she was later told not to tell anyone. It was really from one of Dad's brothers, who had bought a whole side of ham on the 'black market'. Josie didn't know where this market was, and she had certainly never seen one painted black!

The only drawback to this lovely tea was the fact that everyone had to eat at least one slice of bread and marge with both the salad and the fruit. It was a rule and Josie used to get it over with by eating the slice of bread first, leaving her free to enjoy the rest of the food.

Mum and Dad used to mutter about people who 'did well' out of the war. Among these, apparently, were Mr and Mrs Smart, the people who lived at the top of the street. Mr Smart owned his own factory and changed what he made into making something for the war effort. No-one knew exactly what it was. They certainly went up in the world. Their old car was replaced by a beautiful big 'posh' car. Sadly Tony and Shirley were sent away to boarding school as weekly boarders. Mr Smart would let the children ride on the 'running board' (as the sides of his posh car were called) and stop for them to get off at the top of the street.

Once Josie went with them to take Shirley back to school. It was very exciting to ride in a car. Josie hadn't been in a car before. The first part of the journey there was interesting, but coming back, when it got dark, it was very boring, and by the time they got home to Josie's house she was fast asleep.

It was Josie's last year at the Infant School. She was now a 'top infant' and one of the 'big girls'. She still had to walk to school, home and back for lunch, and home at the end of school. It was a long walk to school. David's mum shared the fetching and carrying. Dad came home for lunch each day on his bike. The children whose mothers were working on the war effort were allowed school dinners, as were those whose dads were away fighting the war. Mum found it difficult to supply interesting meals because of the shortage of food and rationing. Irish stew (boiled sheep's ribs and vegetables) was a staple as were rabbit stew and rabbit pie. Josie quite enjoyed 'Pom', the dried potato powder that they used. She found it great for making islands in the gravy and 'bombing' them with pieces of carrot or swede, and was always getting told off for 'messing about' with her food. Josie also liked the rubbery processed cheese that took the place of 'real cheese', though Mum and Dad didn't.

Food was not easy; rations were small and everybody was encouraged to grow as much as possible. All around were posters saying 'Dig for Victory', encouraging them to help the war effort. Josie's dad always grew lots anyway because they had a big garden, but some people didn't even have gardens, so they were encouraged to get allotments, patches of land that were split into sections. Areas which didn't have spare land had to use bits of the park or the gardens of a historic house to provide their allotments.

Josie and her family were very used to sleeping in the Morrison shelter. It just became part of normal life, though soon they had reason to bless it.

It had been a particularly heavy bombing raid that night. Josie had got used to sleeping through the drone of planes and even though the siren disturbed her, she soon went back to sleep again. Mostly the bombs were in the distance; however, that night the planes seemed lower and louder and finally there was the most enormous bang you could imagine. Josie sat up with a start. 'That sounded close!' said Dad.

Come daylight, they saw to their horror that the Proctors' house, the one behind theirs facing onto the next road, had completely disappeared, except for one wall which still had wallpaper flapping forlornly and furniture teetering on the edge.

There were many workers on the site in the early light. Josie tagged on behind Dad when he went round to see if there was anything he could do. He spoke briefly to the men. A small black patent shoe lay dustily amid the rubble. Josie swallowed hard and said in a little voice, 'That's one of Nina's best shoes. Shall I get it for her?'

Gently Dad said to her, 'Nina isn't going to need shoes anymore.'

Josie's tummy gave a big lurch and turned over. Suddenly the war wasn't just soldiers killing each other in another country anymore and, for the first time, Josie realised she could be killed too and was very, very frightened.

They were all very sad at the loss of the Proctors. It was thought that a German bomber plane had jettisoned his last bomb on his way back from the city. They had been bombing the munitions factories where British weapons and bombs were being made. The Proctors had not been using their shelter. It made Dad even more determined to always use their shelter.

Chapter 6

That Christmas it was Dad's brother's turn to host the big family Christmas party. They spent Christmas day quietly at home. Going to church on Christmas day was fun because all the children were allowed to bring their best new present. The air was crisp and cold, breath came out of mouths like smoke. Little girls pushed prams, boys rode bikes (black regulation ones). Josie had one as well and rode it on the pavement with great pride. It was practice for the next day, when she and Mum and Dad were going to cycle all the way to Uncle Bob's for the party.

Boxing Day came and the trio set out on their bikes in a convoy: Dad at the front, Josie in the middle and Mum bringing up the rear. It was a long way, the other side of town, and Josie's legs ached, but there was no other way to get there. There were no buses over Christmas, very few people had cars and, if you did have one, petrol was rationed.

Uncle Bob and Auntie Joan always gave a marvellous party. It began with an exchange of presents. Josie was disgusted by her gift. It was yet another box of embroidered hankies. Auntie Joan said that when Josie stopped losing all the previous year's hankies, she would get her something different. Josie and hankies didn't get on. Josie's mum had given up and equipped Josie each day with a piece of rag, which Josie invariably lost. In the end, she pinned the rag on a piece of tape into Josie's pocket and changed it daily.

There was a wonderful array of party food. Auntie Joan loved cooking and you could tell. She excelled at it and, in spite of the rationing, it was always a great feast. Mum and Dad thought that the black market was responsible for many of the ingredients, but everyone was enjoying the food so much that they didn't question it!

After tea came the games. For one game, several people were sent to wait outside. There was a lot of whispering and giggling and a rustling of paper. People were called back in, one at a time. When Josie went in, it was pitch black. She was told that she had to feel the legs of all the people sitting there and tell who it was. What Josie didn't know was that there was a stuffed stocking in place of one of the legs, which came off when you pulled the leg.

Josie felt the legs. She reached Mum, she recognised her giggle. Josie pulled and off came the leg. Josie screamed; she really believed she had pulled off her mother's leg! The lights went on. Mum said, 'It's all right. It's not real. It's only a game,' but Josie sobbed uncontrollably and could not be comforted.

The next game was more fun. A person was blindfolded and had to stand on a special square piece of board. Then a book was pressed down on their head and they were told they were going to float up to the ceiling. Then the person began to move up. They were told to reach up and touch the ceiling. Josie did, and was amazed to find herself so high up. Then she was told to take off the blindfold and saw she was only inches off the floor, lifted by the men, while someone else held a big book over her to fool her it was the ceiling. It certainly worked and Josie enjoyed watching it work on other people who came in to 'fly to the ceiling'.

After lots more party games, all the guests had to do a 'party piece', a piece to entertain the others. Mum stood on a chair and recited Wordsworth's poem 'Daffodils' – 'I wandered lonely as a cloud' – which she had learned at school. Someone played the ukulele. Others sang. Josie sweetly sang 'Away in a Manger' to the accompaniment of oohs and ahs from the aunties and uncles.

Then came the bit that Josie liked best: the singsong round the piano. Uncle Bob couldn't read music but could play anything anyone asked for by ear. It went on and on until everyone was gasping for a cup of tea. After tea, mince pies and other food left from earlier, people began to drift off home. Mum and Dad were cycling home, but Josie was sharing a bed with her girl cousin, Angela, and Mum and Dad were coming back for her in daylight.

The girls were tired, but went on talking and giggling, in spite of it being well after midnight, until commanded by an exasperated Uncle Bob to 'shut up and go to sleep'. So they did and thus ended one of the best Christmas parties ever!

Chapter 7

Something strange was happening to Mum. Josie just couldn't fathom it out. Mum was getting fatter and always putting her feet up. Then David's mum did a lot more of the fetching and carrying to school.

One day Mum and Dad took Josie aside and told her that Mum was having a baby. 'A little sister, please,' requested Josie.

Dad chuckled. 'I'm afraid we don't have any choice in the matter. God decides.'

Mum was going to a nursing home to have the baby. Josie had been born at home. Josie wanted Mum to have her sister or brother at home so she could watch, but Mum said she wouldn't be allowed to anyway. Mum went away and left Josie with Dad. Josie thought they managed pretty well, but she was longing to have her mum back.

The baby was born. It was a boy. Josie wanted the baby to be called Tony, only to find he was being called James because it was a family name.

Dad brought Mum home from the nursing home in a taxi. She came in carrying a big white bundle, which was placed in Josie's old pram, which had been cleaned and polished until it shone.

Josie crept up to the pram and peered in. She could hardly see the baby's face for the big shawl. She parted the shawl to look. His eyes opened and he took one look and screamed. Josie fled. He went on crying and crying and crying. Josie cried too. In fact every time James cried, Josie cried as well. It made Mum and Dad laugh. 'Why are *you* crying?' said Dad.

'He's sad or he's hurt,' said Josie.

'He's hungry,' said Mum. Then she fed him and Josie thought that was absolutely amazing. He went straight back to sleep, all milky and cuddly, and Josie was allowed to hold him.

Josie told everyone at school about her baby brother and they all wanted to see him. Josie begged Mum to wheel him down to school one day when she came to collect her. Josie was really proud of her little brother as all her friends crowded round the pram to gaze at him.

James was quite the loudest baby anyone had ever come across. Neighbours reported being woken up by James's crying night after night. 'If it's not Hitler, it's James,' they grumbled.

Bath time was Josie's favourite time. Mum would put up the clothes horse covered with towels in the kitchen in front of the big black range. Then she would fill the bath that Josie used on Friday night in front of the living room fire for her bath. They had a perfectly good bath upstairs but it was very cold up there.

Josie looked with interest the first time James was undressed for his bath. So that's what boys looked like – quite different from her. 'I'm glad I'm tidy,' said Josie with satisfaction. 'I wouldn't like all those "bits".'

At school Josie told all her friends about James in the bath. They wanted to come and see. Josie asked Mum if she would bath James at teatime so her friends could come and watch after school, and Mum agreed. Then Josie had a brainwave. What if she were to charge them to come. Twelve children at one penny each. That would be a whole shilling for Josie to spend.

The first six children managed to find a penny for the entertainment, and Josie had others on the 'waiting list'. Everyone enjoyed watching and James for his part enjoyed showing off, splashing and chuckling. All the little girls who didn't have brothers of their own agreed with Josie, saying that they were glad they were 'tidy' too. Unfortunately Mum refused to give a repeat performance and Josie's source of income dried up.

Mum used to wheel James down to the chemist in the village to be weighed. (The clinic was in the next town.) A special morning was set aside for the purpose, and in the holidays Josie could come too. There were always at least six prams outside.

James didn't like being weighed. He had all his warm clothes removed and, instead of a lovely warm bath to play in, he was placed on some cold metal scales on only a piece of paper, so he screamed as only James could. All the other mothers covered their own or their baby's ears. How could one small baby make so much noise?

Back in the pram outside, James's cries subsided. Josie knew that all the other mothers would be commenting on *her* baby brother. Their babies were lying quietly superior in their prams.

Josie went up to each pram and blew in its baby occupant's face until it began to cry. She soon had a symphony of crying babies. Mums hurried out of the chemist's where they had been gossiping to see a smiling Josie and a serenely sleeping James, the only one of the babies *not* to be crying.

Mum brought James down to the school one afternoon to take him to the doctor's to be immunised. To Josie's surprise they didn't go into the waiting room as Josie would have done. James was wheeled down the side path. Mum knocked on the doctor's window. The doctor opened up his sash window and James was handed through to be returned again, screaming loudly, after the injection. 'Good pair of lungs,' commented the doctor.

'Everyone says that,' sighed Mum.

Granny loved James, but Josie believed she was her favourite and so she was not surprised that Granny did not come round as often. 'It's because I'm at school all day,' said Josie confidently. 'She misses me.'

Then Granny stopped coming altogether. 'I'm afraid Granny is not very well,' said Mum.

Josie supposed it was like the cold she had just had, so she was not too worried. Then she heard that Granny was in hospital. Granny didn't come for ages and ages and they didn't go for any visits to Gran's and Josie missed her more and more. She was very relieved and joyful when she heard that Granny was out of hospital.

It was Josie's birthday and there was unusually to be a family party to celebrate and Granny was coming. 'Hooray!' Josie shrieked.

Mum took her to one side and said quietly, 'Granny is still very ill and she's only coming for a short time and no-one, especially you Josie, is to excite her.'

Granny arrived at teatime in a taxi and Grandad and her sons helped her into the house. Josie was shocked to see how ill Granny still looked, but she was out of hospital, so she must be getting better, so Josie forgot all about being quiet and good and behaved as if everything was normal. She shouted and bounced, and kept talking to Granny and wanting to sit on her knee as usual. All the other relatives had been quiet and gentle with Granny, but after a while Granny decided it was time to go home. Josie was disappointed and said so, but was shushed by everyone else. After very emotional and tearful goodbyes, the taxi came and Granny was gone.

That was the last time Josie saw Granny. A couple of weeks later, Dad wanted to talk to Josie alone in the front room. Mum was nowhere to be seen when Dad broke the news that Granny had died. Josie started to cry. 'Don't cry,' said Dad. 'It's your mum's mum and she's very upset too, and you'll make it worse if she sees you crying.'

Josie tried hard to pull herself together. 'But it's my fault,' she sobbed. 'Mum asked me to be quiet and sensible and I wasn't. I killed Granny.'

'No,' said Dad. 'She was old and very ill. She would be so sad if she knew you were blaming yourself. Be a good girl and try to stay cheerful for Mum's sake.' So Josie tried as hard as she could when Mum was around and only cried under the covers in her bed at night, but alas no amount of crying was going to bring Granny back.

The last term at the infants' school soon arrived. The top class infants were going to put on a play before they left, for the whole school and their parents. Their teacher adapted a book called *Ameliaranne and the Green Umbrella*. It was about a little girl going to a party. All her brothers and sisters as well as Ameliaranne had been invited to a birthday party. The brothers and sisters got measles and couldn't go and Ameliaranne promised that she would go and bring them all some party food back. She took her green umbrella with her because it looked like rain. Ameliaranne put lots of party food in the green umbrella to take home. When it came to home time it began to rain and the hostess of the party insisted that she put up the umbrella for Ameliaranne. She was showered with food and had a lot of explaining to do, as well as apologising.

To her delight, Josie was chosen to be Ameliaranne. She had a great time getting as much fun out of the situations as she could, and everyone roared with laughter as the food (provided by her mum) fell out of the umbrella. It was very satisfying making people laugh. Josie remembered losing her sailor skirt at the pantomime; she had enjoyed hearing the audience laugh there too. She decided that she would quite like to make people laugh for a job when she grew up, but most of all she wished Granny could have been there to see her triumph.

Chapter 8

It was time to go 'up' to the junior school. Josie thought the 'Juniors' was very scary. It was just down the road from the 'Infants', next to the church, and was a much older building. It was the original school for the area, catering from infants to school leavers in earlier years. It looked dark and forbidding, with very high windows that she couldn't even look through. It seemed like a prison.

On the first morning both mums (hers and David's) came with them to the door, but were not allowed inside.

The children sat at double desks with a shelf below for books, and a shared wooden bench to sit on which was joined to the desk. They all faced the front, where the teacher's high desk stood. They were asked to write down their names and addresses. Josie quickly did it and looked round at everyone still industriously writing, so she added the county, the country, the continent, the world and the universe to her address. It was a mistake! Her teacher told her so when she held up Josie's paper to show the class what *not* to do.

Playtime came and Josie was horrified to find that she couldn't even play with David and the other boys. The boys had to go to the boys' playground. The girls' playground was at the other side of the school. Josie stood in the doorway to the boys' yard looking longingly at her friends, until she was shooed away and sent to the girls' yard.

The girls were all doing 'girly' things and it looked very boring. She stood alone in the girls' yard, feeling very forlorn. She was not very good at ball catching (or throwing) and she couldn't do handstands against the wall; she was only any good at holding the end of the skipping rope, not skipping *in* it. Josie could run fast and climb high, but there was no opportunity to do either in the girls' yard. 'Come on, Ginger, come and turn the rope,' shouted someone. Josie hated being called 'Ginger' but she went and joined in.

In the classroom the girls sat in pairs at the double desks at one side of the classroom and the boys on the other. She began life at the back of the classroom, but frequent 'talking' soon got her moved to the front! Right under the eyes of Miss Frazer. Miss Frazer had a horrible habit of wandering round the classroom armed with a wooden ruler while the children were working. Josie could feel her brooding presence behind her, followed by a sharp rap on the knuckles if the sum was wrong. Even worse was when she failed to hear Miss Frazer approaching, only to jump out of her skin when the ruler flashed down on her hand. Most dreaded were the mental arithmetic tests. Josie was usually several sums behind and couldn't hear the next question because she was still trying to work out a previous one.

Now she was a Junior and with a baby brother at home to occupy Mum, Josie was allowed to take herself to school. David called for her in the morning and they were joined by the Price boys, Peter and Robert, and 'Douglas down the road'. They always meant to get to school on time and quite often did, but there were always so many distractions on the long journey and the boys and Josie were frequently found lining up outside the Head's room when he returned from taking assembly, waiting to be caned for lateness. Assembly was so dull; they always seemed to be singing 'All Things Bright and Beautiful', varied occasionally by 'Onward Christian Soldiers' or 'There is a Green Hill' at Easter. Missing assembly was no great loss.

An advantage of being a Junior was to have greater freedom. Josie and the boys could go off exploring the Common and the only thing that drove them home was hunger. They often ate at each other's houses. All the grown-ups were so busy that no-one seemed to notice they were missing.

Coming home from school was good as well because there was no cane waiting if they were late, but Josie didn't like to be too late because of Children's Hour on the radio (or 'wireless' as every-one called it). She loved Larry the Lamb and his friends in Toyland. 'Out with Romany' made her feel she was really out in the countryside. Uncle Mac and Auntie Vi were her friends and she was very excited by the stories of the Boy Detectives – Norman and Henry Bones.

Mum told Josie that there was a thing called television before the war, when you could see the people who were talking. Mum found Josie peering into the radiogram where it was lit up, trying to see the miniature people who were performing, and had to break the news to Josie that she was not going to see television that way!

Josie kept missing time at school with things called 'tonsils'. They were at the back of her throat and were often very swollen and sore. It was decided that Josie's tonsils and adenoids were to be removed in an operation at the hospital. Josie was told that it wouldn't hurt because she would be asleep when the tonsils were taken out. She was also promised ice cream after the operation (which she couldn't get normally) as a treat and a reward.

All went well to start with. Josie sat bravely in the waiting room and chatted to the other children who were also having the operation. One by one they were taken away for their operation. As they went for their operation, most of them were crying. Josie vowed that she would not cry and when the trolley arrived she smiled cheerfully and they asked her if she wanted to climb on and have a ride. Josie dutifully climbed on the trolley and waved goodbye to Mum and the trolley was wheeled across the waiting area and began to climb up a ramp. Josie changed her mind. She shouted loudly, 'I don't want to ride on your trolley,' and began to climb off. The nurse tried to keep her on, and the porter pushed faster. It ended in an undignified scramble with Josie shouting and fighting every bit of the way. The anaesthetist asked her to breathe into her mask and count to ten. 'I don't want to breathe into your mask and I'm *not* counting to ten.' Mum said she could hear her complaining from the waiting room. So much for bravery!

When she came round in the ward there was someone waiting with a big dish of ice cream but her throat hurt so much that she couldn't swallow it. What a waste! Josie didn't exactly cover herself with glory on that day, but when she got home next day she greedily ate the ice cream that Mr Sharp had managed to get for her. It was very enjoyable, but not worth having her tonsils out.

Back at school, the operation became more and more dramatic as Josie related it and in the end it bore no resemblance to the actual event.

Miss Frazer decided to reorganise the classroom and all the girls were paired up. Josie was even more of a misfit with the girls than before she had been away from school. Miss Frazer had a problem. Standing before her were Josie and Gloria Wilde, the only other left-over girl.

Gloria came from a large family living near the school in a small house. They had no bathroom or indoor toilet and, to be honest, Gloria smelled bad. None of the other girls would go near her and Miss Frazer couldn't blame them. Josie still didn't have much of a sense of smell after her tonsils and adenoids had been removed so, in the last double desk, Miss Frazer put Josie and Gloria. Josie smiled encouragingly and Gloria smiled back. They quite liked each other. After all, thought Josie, I get very dirty when I'm playing out.

Gloria invited Josie to come home with her one day after school. Josie couldn't believe it when she walked into Gloria's house. It was so small, damp and smelly, just one room and a scullery downstairs. Gloria could not remember exactly how many brothers and sisters she had, but there were certainly a lot of them. There were two bedrooms upstairs and two attic bedrooms above that and it seemed they had to share beds (top and tail) as well as rooms.

Gloria's mother gave Josie a drink of weak tea in a jam jar. They had newspaper on the table instead of a cloth, and there was no sign of any toys or books. Josie couldn't believe how little Gloria had. All the way home Josie thought how lucky she was to have her mum and dad (Josie never ever saw Gloria's dad) and a nice house, books and toys, and she resolved to bring something for Gloria.

Josie had a favourite doll she called Rosemary with a china head, hands and feet and a stuffed body, who wore a pretty, frilly party dress. Rosemary had been her doll for as long as she could remember, and because she was breakable she was played with only occasionally.

Mum saw Josie carrying the doll to school the next day. 'Where are you taking that doll?' asked Mum.

'To school to show everybody,' Josie answered truthfully.

'It's very fragile, Josie. I'm not sure you should take it.'

'I'll give it to the teacher to look after until home time,' promised Josie and in the end Mum agreed.

Gloria couldn't believe the beauty of the doll. Her eyes grew wide with wonder. 'Can I hold her?' she begged.

'That's what she's here for,' smiled Josie.

Gloria played with Rosemary every playtime and in between time Rosemary sat on the top of Miss Frazer's cupboard.

Home time arrived. Friday – the weekend. Rosemary was handed down to Josie, who gave Gloria a last cuddle of the doll. Suddenly Josie said, 'Would you like to keep her?'

Gloria's eyes grew wide. 'Yes, yes, of course.'

Josie thought of all the other dolls and soft animals she had at home and, as a big Junior girl, she had little time for dolls because she was too busy exploring and having adventures. She could very well manage without Rosemary.

Gloria walked home proudly carrying the doll. Josie ran to catch up with the boys.

When Josie walked into the kitchen, the first thing her mother said was, 'Where's Rosemary?'

'I gave her to Gloria,' Josie replied.

'You did what?' Her mother couldn't believe her ears. 'First thing you do when you get to school on Monday is to ask for her back.'

'I can't do that!' Josie was horrified. 'You can't ask for presents back.'

'Well, I can,' said her mother grimly.

Nothing else was said. Friday tea was eaten in silence and disapproval. Normally Josie liked Friday nights. It was bath night and detective Paul Temple was on the radio, while the bath took place in front of the fire. Josie also had her hair washed in black Derbac soap and then nit-combed over a large sheet of brown paper. Mum began to comb, then she began to shriek, 'Look at those things!' They were lice that fell out of Josie's hair all over the brown paper. They were at different stages of development and her hair was full of nits (the eggs), clinging very tightly to individual hairs.

Josie's mum was very upset; it was considered a disgrace to have nits. If the nit nurse found a child with nits, that child was excluded from school until the clinic had checked that they were clear.

'That does it!' said Josie's mum. 'I'm going to write to Miss Frazer.'

Josie spent all that weekend having her hair washed and nit-combed until her mum was satisfied that both nits and lice had gone.

On Monday morning Josie presented Miss Frazer with the letter. It was to say that Josie was not to sit next to Gloria and why. Miss Frazer shuddered. She could now see the active lice crawling about on Gloria's head. Miss Frazer filled in a card and sent Gloria to the clinic attached to the infant school. Gloria departed in tears; she knew why she was going to the clinic. Miss Frazer had no option but to ask for another desk in an already crowded classroom so that Gloria could sit on her own.

When Josie arrived home at teatime, the first thing Josie's mother said was, 'Have you changed your place?'

'Yes.'

'And where is the doll?'

'I'm not going to ask for it back,' said Josie. 'Gloria is too upset already, and anyway I've grown out of dolls and it's mine to give away.'

Josie's mum, who was a kind person really, nodded agreement. She was not happy about Josie's decision but, as it was Josie's doll, it was Josie's decision to make.

Chapter 9

Beyond David's garden and the stagnant green pond was a deep, dark wood. It was guarded by a barbed wire fence and a notice which read: 'Keep out. Trespassers will be prosecuted.' Josie could now read the notice and, having ascertained what 'trespassers' and 'prosecuted' meant, did not attempt to enter the wood. That all changed, however, when someone cut the wire with wire-cutters and left a gap big enough to get through.

'Probably poachers,' said David knowledgeably. David and Josie were first through the gap to explore the dark world inside.

All the children who walked to school with Josie and David were boys. They had all been enjoying the *Just William* by Richard Compton read out to them at school. The boys in *Just William* were a gang; a good gang, but nevertheless a gang. In the book, William was the leader and Ginger his second in command. David became the leader of *his* gang, and Ginger Josie became his deputy. Peter and Robert Price, 'Douglas down the street', John and Tony became the members of David's gang.

Having explored the beginning of the wood themselves, David and Josie rounded up the gang to go back in with them. They were all a bit scared but no-one was going to show it. 'We should build a den,' said David, 'as our headquarters.'

'What with?' asked Peter.

'Any materials to hand,' said David grandly.

There was a shout from Josie. 'I've found a load of old bricks and stones over here. It looks as if there may have been something built here at one time.'

'We could put the bricks and stones for foundations,' said David, 'then put the wood and branches on top.'

The gang set to work. It was a hot and sweaty job but at last there was the basis of a den.

The gang visited their den after school and at the weekend and brought bits and pieces from home to make it more comfortable, an old mat, some cushions. Josie even brought a discarded vase from the shed at home and put wild flowers in it, which was jeered at by the boys. They begged food and drink to 'have a picnic' and ate them in the den. It had a low roof of branches and leaves. It became a real home from home and was a total secret.

It was like the wartime posters, 'Walls have ears'. No-one in the gang spoke about it, especially at school.

They arrived one day to find that things had been disturbed. They knew straightaway that someone else had found the gap in the wire. They didn't have long to wonder before some boys from a neighbouring street arrived. 'That's our den,' they said.

'No, it isn't,' said David. 'We got here first and we made the den.'

'Fight you for it,' said the rival gang leader, who was a bigger, older boy from their school. He threw the first stone.

A battle ensued. David's gang took up a defensive position behind the walls of the den. They had to dispense with the roof to stand up behind the walls. From behind that they could throw bits of the wall and sticks from the roof at their rivals. David's gang had more ammunition than their rivals and after a stone had made contact with a rival's cheek, causing blood to flow, the opposition retired, defeated. 'We've won!' David's gang shouted.

Their victory didn't last long. When they returned the next day, the enemy was in occupation and they had lost their prized den.

Josie came back on her own to see if she could find another good place to build a den. Suddenly amid the tangle of undergrowth she saw a building. It was two storeys high and painted green and white. The ground floor windows were all boarded up, but there were lots of little holes above on the upstairs. This might do, thought Josie, but she couldn't move the boards to get in. Even when she came back with the gang, they couldn't get inside. 'Nice try, Ginger,' said Douglas.

'What is it?' asked Peter.

'I don't know,' said David. 'Let's ask at home, but we must not give anything away.'

Josie asked her dad, who had always lived in the area. 'The wood belongs to the Big House,' he told her. 'It's part of the estate. That building was a pigeon loft. Right on the edge of the wood and painted like that to show the racing pigeons the way home. Before they built our houses there were fields everywhere.'

'What happened?' asked Josie, wide-eyed.

'The war happened; the First World War took all the male staff to fight. Sir Christopher sold some of the fields for housing to fund the upkeep of the house. Then the second (this war) took men and lots of women too to work in munitions – you know, the gun and bomb factories. No more shooting of game in the woods. No more pigeons. The formal gardens are growing food and the Hall has been taken over for the soldiers to recover from their injuries.'

'Will it ever go back to how it was?'

'I doubt it,' said Dad. 'It depends if we win this war.'

Josie was shocked. 'Mum said we would win. She said that right was on our side and right always won through.'

'There, there,' soothed Dad. 'She's probably right; she usually is. She has right on her side.'

Josie related all this to the boys. They were really interested in everything she told them. The children sang songs about Hitler and the Germans. They sang, 'It's raining, it's pouring, Hitler went to Goring. He lost his pants in the middle of France; now he can't get up in the morning,' which were words the children made up. They knew lots of wartime songs. Some were known and sung by everybody, like 'The Quartermaster's Store', 'Kiss Me Goodnight, Sergeant Major', 'Run Rabbit, Run' and 'Knees Up, Mother Brown'. Others were known only by the fighting troops because they had very rude words and Dad said they were too rude for women and children to listen to.

The gang stopped using the wood to play and went instead down the road onto the Common. There was a farm at the end of Josie's road, with a duck pond right up to the walls of the farmhouse. Josie used to go with Mum to feed the ducks when she was younger. The farm was the estate farm and belonged to the Big House. There was a lane going past the farm and onto the Common. Some of the fields near the farm had cows in them and were fenced in, but the rest of the Common was open land and anybody could walk there.

It was a very large Common and seemed endless to the children. If you kept on walking, eventually you came to a small group of cottages that was a tiny hamlet with no proper road. There were not any trespass notices to stop the gang and they practically lived there that summer.

A new den was made in the bottom of a sprawling hawthorn hedge. It was lined with dried grass and totally hidden by green leaves, and earlier by the sweet-smelling blossom, which Josie thought was the loveliest smell on earth.

One day a young couple came and sat in the shade of their hedge, while the gang was inside the den. The couple were not speaking English; they were talking in a foreign language. The gang sat tight, holding their breath so as not to be discovered. Eventually the young man and woman, who had been poring over a printed book and making notes in a notebook, stopped what they were doing and exchanged a few kisses – to stifled giggles from the boys – and stood up, dropping the notebook as they did so.

When the couple had gone out of earshot, the gang pounced on the book and took it into the dim recesses of the den. It was full of foreign words. 'It must be German,' declared Josie. 'They must be German spies.'

'What should we do?' asked Peter.

'We should take the notebook to the police,' said Robert.

'No,' said David, excited. 'We must trail them, so the police know where to go to catch them.'

'But they've gone,' protested Josie.

'Then we'll run fast and catch up with them,' said David. 'They can't have got off the Common yet. We'll soon find them.'

The gang set off in hot pursuit, running as fast as they could and in full view. Soon they caught up with the spies. They slowed down, split up and melted into the trees and bushes. The couple were still talking in a foreign language, but occasionally they seemed to sense that they were being followed and glanced back.

It was all very exciting. The gang really felt they were taking part in the war.

A problem arose when the couple separated and went their different ways. David signalled for Josie to come with him and follow the girl, and for the other three to follow the young man.

Josie and David followed the girl all the way to the main road when, to their disappointment, she got on a bus going into town. They went back, just as Peter, Robert and Douglas came into view, breathless from their tracking. 'He went into one of the cottages on the farm,' said Peter. 'We'll show you if you like.'

'All right,' agreed David, 'but we'd better make sure he doesn't see us.'

Although they were very careful, he did see them as he opened his cottage door. The gang all walked on past the farm as their quarry watched them.

'We've still got the notebook,' said David. 'Perhaps we'd better give it to the police.'

'Not yet,' objected Robert. 'This is great fun, don't let's stop yet.'

'They may be plotting an invasion,' worried David. 'It's the only right thing to do.'

'Tell you what,' said Josie, 'why don't some of us watch the cottage, while someone else goes for the police.'

Suddenly the door opened again. The young man locked up and set off at a good pace. David guessed where he was heading – the meeting place where he had been seen with the girl. 'Go and get the police,' said David. 'Bring them to our den, while I follow him. You lot wait here in case he comes back.'

'Be careful,' said Josie as she set off for the police as fast as her legs would carry her.

David was right. The man did go back to where he had been yesterday and began frantically searching.

David got as close as he could, creeping ever nearer. The man turned round suddenly and pounced on David, grabbing him by the arm, pouring out a torrent of words in an unintelligible language. Fortunately, at that moment two policemen arrived with Josie and the notebook in tow. David was released and the police held on to his attacker. His attacker spoke in very heavily accented and halting English, explaining that this boy had been spying on him with some other children, including that girl, and he wanted it to stop.

The police had been on foot patrol when Josie found them. All of them were escorted back to the main road to the nearest police box, where a police car was called and they were taken to the local police station.

Josie and David sat in a room with a police lady, wondering what was happening. Eventually a senior police officer appeared. He sat down opposite to speak to them. He congratulated them on being so alert, but told them that they should have turned the notebook in straightaway.

It seemed that the young man was Dutch and was working at the farm. The girl was his girlfriend and he had been teaching her to speak his language because they wanted to marry after the war was over. The notebook was full of words which she had been trying to learn so as to communicate better with each other. They had both been talking French, which was a language that they both knew a little, having had lessons in school.

After that, both sets of parents arrived to collect their children. Josie and David were both given separate scoldings from their respective parents, and were then driven home by the police in two police cars.

When they told the police how Peter, Robert and 'Douglas down the street' had all been involved in trying to catch the 'spies', they, together with David and Josie, all received thank you letters for their efforts in trying to catch the spies, but it was suggested very politely that if a similar situation ever arose again, they should bring in some adults first before tackling things themselves.

Chapter 10

Now Josie was getting older and, her mother thought, 'more responsible', she was to be trusted to shop on the way home from school. Mum wanted Josie to bring a loaf of bread and gave her a shiny silver sixpence to buy the bread and bring home the change. She was also told not to break bits off the crust to eat on the way home!

To go to the corner shop that sold the bread, Josie had to take a different route home. The boys wouldn't come with her because it was further to go, so she set off on the detour to get the shopping, having first had a game of 'catch' with them all.

When she reached the shop, she put her hand in her pocket for the sixpence but it was not there. It must have fallen out when they were playing. Josie retraced her steps, eyes fixed on the ground, all the way back to where they had parted. It *must* be here, thought Josie, becoming more frantic with worry.

What will Mum say? She even got down on her hands and knees on the cobbles and in the gutters to try to find it. Perhaps it had rolled down a drain. Tears rolled down Josie's cheeks. 'The first time Mum's trusted me to shop,' she said to herself, 'and I've let her down.'

Josie didn't know how long she had been looking and crying until she realised it was almost dark. She sat on the edge of the pavement, feet in the gutter, and sobbed. Suddenly there was a hand on her shoulder and a familiar voice said her name. It was Dad. He had come home from work to find Mum upset and worrying about Josie and come looking for her. Big girl though she was, he picked her up and hugged her tightly. Josie buried her head in his shoulder and in shuddering sobs tried to explain about the lost sixpence. 'There, there,' soothed Dad. 'Not to worry. *You're* more important than a lost sixpence. We thought we had lost *you*.' He took Josie into the warm light of the corner shop. He bought a loaf and with the change and some sweet coupons bought some sweets for Josie. She felt warm and cosy and loved inside and out as she trotted home beside Dad, to an equally warm welcome from Mum who had been 'worried sick' at her absence.

The children were all enjoying school this year with Miss Price as their teacher. She was not as strict as

Miss Frazer, so no more rapped knuckles. She seemed to like the children too, especially David and Josie, who were both good at English. They were also good at telling stories. She always read or told a story at the end of the day and sometimes she would ask Josie or David to tell the class a story instead. The class noticed that she always got on with her marking when Josie or David were storytelling, but no-one minded because they both told such exciting stories.

The only blot on Josie's horizon was Mr Dacre. He was old and grey and took the top class and ruled them with a rod of iron. He also took boys' PE and handwork in the other Junior classes. The dreaded handwork lesson loomed over Josie all week. They spent the entire autumn term making a calendar. They measured the picture, they measured and drew a square for the picture to go in. They measured the tab and measured and drew a square for the tab to go in. Josie was rubbish at ruling. You could tell the ruling was inaccurate just by looking and Josie was constantly being derided for her lack of ability in measuring.

Mr Dacre was the only male teacher left at the school; the others had been 'called up' or volunteered to go and fight in the war. Mr Dacre was too old to go. He had fought in the First World War and had a limp from being wounded in action.

Another good thing about being older was that the children were allowed to go without an adult on the bus to the town for the Saturday morning cinema show. Josie was given a shilling pocket money on Saturday to go to the show with her friends. After the cinema (which cost sixpence), they went to the library and changed their books. (They were only allowed one book each.) Then they spent their change and sweet coupons. They always went upstairs on the bus because they got on and off the bus at its terminus. The terminus in town was beside a huge water tank. Josie had heard about swimming baths before the war, but they had all been closed down. Floors were erected over the pool and Saturday evening dances were held there. Josie had once been to a dance with Mum and Dad but she had been scared that the floor might collapse and she would fall into the water beneath and drown. Mum and Dad had laughed at her and said the pool had been drained. When Josie had asked about the big tanks that had been erected in the streets of the town, she had been told they were for the war, but no-one had explained what they were to do in the war.

Josie thought that they were replacement swimming pools. From the upstairs of the bus, she could see into the tanks. The water was black and they looked very deep and cold with bits of rubbish floating on top. 'I'm not going swimming in there;

it's too deep and dirty,' Josie declared. She was greeted with hoots of laughter.

David said, 'They are for the Fire Brigade to put the fires out in town when they've been hit by bombs.'

I'm still not swimming in there after the war, thought Josie stubbornly.

One day Josie definitely didn't feel at all well. She went to school, but when she returned she felt dreadful. Mum put her hand on her burning forehead. 'To bed with you,' she said. 'I'll call the doctor.'

I must be dying, thought Josie; Mum wouldn't pay for the doctor to come unless it was serious.

The kindly family doctor, who had looked after Josie since she was a baby, was quite concerned too. 'It's a very severe dose of measles; she's got it badly. There are many complications you must watch out for. I'll call in again tomorrow after morning surgery.'

I must be really ill, thought Josie; two home visits for Mum and Dad to pay for.

Indeed Josie was very ill for quite a while. When she was beginning to feel better, Mum had a job to keep her still. The doctor said she must rest in a darkened room and not read or draw, which was very boring. Most of all, Josie missed her friends, who had not been allowed to visit in case they caught it.

There was a shout from the back garden. It was her friends. Josie ran to the window and, forgetting all instructions, pulled aside the blackout curtains. The light hurt her eyes, but she blinked and waved excitedly to her friends before Mum shooed them away and told Josie in no uncertain terms to close the curtains and get back into bed immediately before too much damage had been done. After that day, Josie's eyes ran a lot and felt very weak and Mum scolded that she had probably damaged them just as the doctor had warned.

Soon Josie was back at school. She didn't say anything at home, but Miss Price noticed that she screwed up her eyes to see the blackboard and moved her to the front. The other children noticed that she always made a beeline for the front rows at the Saturday morning cinema club.

Every year an optician came into school to test the children's eyes. The testing took place in the school hall. Josie looked at the card with all the letters on and realised that she might have a problem seeing them when she reached the reading position.

The children sat on chairs all down the side of the hall whilst waiting their turn to read the letters. Josie had a flash of inspiration; she would learn the letters while she was sitting near the test card as she moved down the side of the hall to the bottom. They were all there in her head because she had a very good memory.

Josie's turn came. She began confidently; she could almost see the first line. Then the next. Then her mind went blank. The tester waited then pointed again. Josie tried. 'No, not *that* line, the line before.'

Josie tried again. Now she was two lines wrong. The tester turned over the card and told her to start again. This time it was a disaster. Josie had never seen those letters before and had no idea. She guessed wildly. The tester beckoned to her to come close. 'You can't really see, can you?' she said.

'No,' said Josie nervously.

'I think we had better see you at the school clinic. You may need glasses. We'll send an appointment card to your mum for her to bring you.'

Josie was horrified. 'I can't wear glasses,' she cried. 'Adventurers don't wear glasses!' She couldn't believe what was happening to her.

Every day at home Josie tried to intercept the postman and foil the attempt to put her into glasses. She didn't manage it. It came second post and Mum was waiting with it in her hand when Josie got home. 'Why didn't you tell me?' Mum said. 'I thought you were having trouble seeing, but you always denied it. This is what happens when you don't obey doctors' orders.'

The appointment time came round and Josie had to see the optician at the school clinic. She had some drops in her eyes before she was examined. This enlarged her pupils but made her eyes hurt, go bleary and run. After a little time she was tested again wearing monster frames. The lady kept changing the lens until Josie could read all the test card. Then they chose the actual frames. There were only three frames but they were free. It wasn't much of a choice because they were all equally hideous. Josie chose the least hideous, which was not saying much. They were small, round and brown and made her look like an owl.

The best thing about the whole experience was being taken to a British Restaurant for lunch. Josie couldn't see what she was eating, but it tasted good.

Fortunately Josie had a short reprieve because she had to wait for the glasses to be made up, but Josie was absolutely dreading the day she had to appear in public with them on.

At last the glasses were ready!

Josie managed to 'forget' her new spectacles a couple of times before Mum realised what she was up to. To make certain that they were going to be worn, Mum accompanied Josie to the front door when the boys called for her to go to school. Their mouths dropped open. Josie had not even warned them that this was going to happen. 'You look like an owl,' gasped David. Josie scowled at him and he took the hint. 'A very *nice* owl,' he continued. The others took the lead and nodded enthusiastically.

'Will you see she keeps them on,' said Josie's mum, 'and tell her teacher she has to wear them.'

The children set off for school with Josie in the middle of the group and no-one mentioned the dreaded glasses until they arrived at the school playground. There was great hilarity at the sight of Josie in her spectacles from the other children in her class, but they all knew better than to say anything. Not so the children from other classes. 'Four Eyes,' they teased, 'Specky Four Eyes, Ginger Specky Four Eyes.'

The group closed protectively around Josie. 'She may be Ginger Specky Four Eyes,' said David angrily, 'but she's *our* Ginger Specky Four Eyes. Leave her alone or you'll be sorry!'

Chapter 11

Josie had become a proficient storyteller during the school year in Miss Price's class. She had become even more of a bookworm too. Josie always had her nose in a book and Mum and Dad became fed up of trying to attract her attention; she was so engrossed she never even heard them speak. She read lots of books at school too.

In the classroom were some small blue books, which were shortened versions of the classics: *Oliver Twist*, *David Copperfield*, *Uncle Tom's Cabin*. She also enjoyed books like *What Katy Did* and *Little Women*, which she read in the full version. Her favourite writer, however, was Enid Blyton. She became hooked on adventure stories, including the Famous Five books and *The Island of Adventure* amongst many others. Pretty soon she was writing her own stories too as well as telling them.

The other thing that Josie liked doing was writing plays, especially pantomimes. She went to a pantomime every year and came home inspired to try and put one on herself. The big bay window in the front room had full length curtains which pulled across leaving the space of the bay inside, just like a real stage. Josie wrote a version of *Cinderella*, making carbon copies for the cast. For *Cinderella* she needed girls, so she had to wheedle some of the girls to take part. The boys flatly refused to take part, saying it was 'girls' stuff'. A couple reluctantly agreed to be 'baddies', but insisted that they had to have weapons and a fight scene. Then people kept dropping out or skipping rehearsals because something better had turned up, or wanted to swap parts because somebody had a better part than them, or fell out with someone and wouldn't act with them. Josie became so frustrated that she finally gave up the idea.

Josie didn't give up on mystery stories, however. She was an avid listener to the wireless. She loved Paul Temple, the detective, and 'The Man in Black', Valentine Dyall, whose deep, deep voice made her feel shivery with fear. Josie would listen in the dark and from under the dining room table to make it even more scary.

Her passion for scary stories even spread into her real life. To get to school it was possible to take a short cut across the church graveyard to save time.

Josie did it quite often. Then she started to make up stories about it being haunted. Some of the old flat stones on top of the tomb-like graves had slipped off a little. Josie started telling everyone that she had seen ghosts of the dead people buried there coming out of the graves. In the autumn term when it got dark early, children became frightened to cross it. Parents complained to the headmaster about this ginger girl who was frightening them. He knew straightaway who it was! He sent for Josie and her parents and said that, while he didn't want to stifle her creativity, it might be better if she kept it to herself and did not frighten the other children.

Josie then began to write her stories down. She filled page after page with them. The longest story she had ever written had filled an exercise book. She thought it was the best she had ever written. In fact, she was so pleased with it, she thought it could be a proper printed book. She found out the address of Hodder & Stoughton (who published the Enid Blyton books), managed to get a large envelope and posted it off. A week later she received a typed envelope with a letter inside that said, 'We acknowledge receipt of your book.'

Josie was thrilled; 'acknowledge', as far as she knew, meant to recognise someone or something and therefore it meant that they recognised Josie as an authoress. She told all her friends that her book was being published and looked forward to receiving her first copy and a cheque, which in her head she had already spent. Alas, she was to be disappointed when her book arrived back, with a very nice letter saying that, although they had enjoyed it, they had a long list of books waiting to be published and didn't have room for hers!

All this time the war had gone on and on and on. Dad had bought some big maps and put them on the wall by the table in the dining room and with drawing pins and coloured wool had followed the progress of the war, especially the ships bringing cargoes from America. America had joined in the war now and sent Britain supplies. The Japanese had attacked all the American ships moored in Pearl Harbour when they were not even involved in the war at that time. Serve them right, thought Josie. America had joined in to fight Hitler too; 'on our side, of course,' Josie told her friends.

Christmas had grown more austere year by year. Fewer and fewer things were available to buy. Everything was rationed and even then Mum had to queue for hours to buy anything. Josie had grown out of all her clothes and shoes and they didn't have enough clothing coupons to replace much. In order to make things go further, the Government had made rules to say that you couldn't have frills, lace, buttons, pockets or pleats. Not that Josie went in for frills and lace.

Mum was very good at sewing and had a sewing machine. She was especially good at remaking her dresses and Dad's shirts into clothing for Josie and James. Mum had a beautiful lavender organdie dress with a full skirt, which she had from before the war began. It was a lovely dress and had enough material in the skirt to make Josie a spectacular party dress.

Josie felt like a princess when she arrived at school for the Christmas party. The girls all clustered round her, admiring her new dress and for once Josie was glad to have them. The boys hadn't even mentioned the dress except to say that they hoped she wasn't going to wear 'that thing' for playing because it would hamper her movements and make playing difficult.

Christmas arrived. It was their turn to have the family to visit this year and Josie was drafted in to help Mum prepare on Christmas Eve. They had managed to get chickens, but they still had on their heads and feet and feathers. Josie didn't like dealing with them and their 'innards'. She plucked feathers for what seemed hours. The feathers floated everywhere in the kitchen and got up Josie's nose. She helped to peel endless potatoes and made crosses in the tops of sprouts from the garden. Mum used her ration of sausages to make small sausage rolls and her bacon ration to go across the tops of the chickens. The giblets were being boiled up to make the gravy, so it was going to be quite a feast. The kitchen was hot and steamy by now and, when the carol singers came, Josie and Mum went into the cold, unheated hall to enjoy them more.

When Christmas Day arrived, it didn't take too long to open presents (many home-made). Josie had her beloved annuals and as many drawing and writing things as her parents had been able to lay their hands on.

After breakfast, Josie was at a bit of a loose end. No church today because of their visitors. Dad was entertaining her little brother and for a while Josie played with him too, so that Dad could move all the furniture ready for the meal. There were a lot of people to sit round the table. Mum was frantically cooking and when Josie popped in, she told her to get out from under her feet!

It was a crisp, hard morning. They had had a sharp frost overnight and not only was the grass white, the little puddles were frozen hard and slippery. It was no use calling for any of her friends; they would either be at church or getting ready for visitors or to go to relatives and would not be allowed out, so Josie went where she always went when nothing exciting was happening. She pulled on her wellingtons and went on the Common.

Josie tried making slides out of the larger puddles. Then she walked until she reached the fenced off pond, some way over the Common. Rumour had it that it was bottomless and that lots of cows had fallen in and drowned and that's why it was fenced off. The fence proved no obstacle to Josie, who was keen to see how hard the water had frozen. She wanted to slide on it, but still had acquired enough common sense by then to test the ice first. She put her foot on it. Good so far. She stood up and put more weight on her leg, then she leaned on it and *crack*, the ice went through, so did Josie's wellington boot, fortunately not followed by Josie, who flung herself back onto the bank of the pond. Of the wellington there was no sign. She used a branch to poke in the water to see if she could find it. It seemed that everyone was right. It really was bottomless. Thank goodness she had not followed the wellington through the ice. Her thick wellington sock was soaking and Josie thought she had better cut her losses and go back home before all the relatives arrived.

Fortunately home was just as hectic as it had been when she set off, so she sneaked in and upstairs, hid her sock, put on her new slippers and went to help lay the table as if nothing had happened.

Mum never did find that second wellington. She searched the house, high and low, puzzled as to how one wellington had managed to vanish.

Josie never told her.

Chapter 12

The cold weather continued after Christmas, concluding in a heavy fall of snow. Snow was great fun when you were with friends – sledging, snowman making, snowball fights. It was not so much fun when enemies were around.

There were a group of boys from the top class (Mr Dacre's) who always persecuted Josie. They never lost an opportunity to call her names, especially when she was on her own. 'Carrots', 'Freckles', 'Ginger' and now 'Ginger Specky Four Eyes' were the epithets flung at her. Josie's mum had taught her 'Sticks and stones may break my bones, but words will never hurt me,' so she just squared her shoulders and tried to ignore them.

In snow, however, it was a different matter. One day, Josie had to stay behind to see Miss Dixon (this year's class teacher). The boys, anxious to be off and to play in the snow, had not waited for her. Josie set off as fast as she could to catch up with them. It was uphill all the way home and Josie's new wellingtons slowed her down (bought a little on the large side to allow for 'growth'). As she reached the main road, her heart sank. The boys who called her names were on the other side of the road. Josie *had* to cross at this point to access the little lane that ran between the vicarage and a neighbouring large house, to the houses where Josie lived and the Common.

Josie couldn't put it off any longer. She crossed the road. 'Here she comes!' the boys jeered. They threw icy balls of snow at her, which hurt as they were very accurate. Then they leapt on her and she fell to the ground. Now they had her captive, snow was put down the back of her neck and in her wellingtons. Josie fought as hard as she could, but was powerless to stop them. Then they lost interest and went.

Josie picked herself up and tried hard not to cry. She was cold and wet and had a large red mark near her eye where an ice ball had hit her. When she reached her street, the boys were still playing out. 'What happened to you?' they asked.

'Mr Dacre's boys,' she said and a large tear she had been unable to stop rolled down her cheek, mingling with the snow.

'We'll get them for this,' vowed David.

'How can we?' asked Peter. 'They're twice the size of us.'

'Leave it with me,' said David grimly. 'I have an idea.'

The next night the boys made sure that they accompanied Josie home and there was no trouble. The day after that, however, David asked Josie if she was brave enough to come home alone again. Josie really didn't want to but she didn't want to appear a 'scare-baby' so she said, 'Yes.'

The long street up the hill to the main road had never seemed so long as Josie trudged up it. When she reached the main road, as before the bully boys were waiting for her. Her heart sank. 'Coming back for more?' they jeered.

Josie crossed the road and, before they could attack her, the place erupted as from many hiding places there came her friends and some even bigger boys. The bullies were rolled in the snow. It was put down their necks and wellingtons and rubbed in their faces and hair. As soon as they were subdued, the biggest boy shouted at them, 'Leave the younger children alone,' as they ran away. It was Guy who lived near them and his friend Nigel and some more of their friends from the grammar school.

'Thanks so much,' gasped Josie.

'Don't mention it. We're not going to let bullies get at you younger children. David told us all about them and asked for our help. It was his idea.'

Guy and Nigel and their friends had once been pupils of their school but had gone on to the grammar school, having won county scholarships.

Talking of scholarships, this was a very important year at school because it was the year that certain children (those with a chance) were chosen to be entered for county scholarships, the Royal Grammar School for the boys and the County High for the girls. Both David and Josie had been chosen to enter. They had come top or near the top in all exams their year had taken. It was very hard work preparing for the scholarship. There was homework every night and extra classes for those entered. The best thing about getting a scholarship as far as Josie was concerned was never having to go into Mr Dacre's class.

In February there came the news that the German Army that had tried to invade Russia were forced to surrender in Stalingrad. Then came the news of a new sort of bomb that was falling on London. It was a 'flying bomb'. A new 'Blitz' was beginning. People called the new bombs doodlebugs and buzz bombs. They were really called the V1 (Vee-one) and later came the V2. They were quieter and did more damage. For the first time since the war began, Josie started to feel really frightened. The doodlebugs began to be dropped in their area. The siren would go. Then Josie heard the drone of the planes as they passed overhead. Josie began to wake when she heard them. She sat bolt upright in the Morrison shelter and listened as the rocket bomb was dropped. The worst bit was when the noise cut out and there was only silence. No-one knew where the bomb was heading in the silence, until the noise of it hitting its target. Dad would say, 'That was near,' or 'Quite far off tonight'. Josie thought that they wouldn't know it was going to hit them – until it did. Then that was the end of life. The buzz bombs were so much more destructive than the old ones. It meant broken nights too and that made them less alert at school the next day.

'Well, at least everyone is in the same boat,' said David ruefully as he yawned for the fifteenth time that morning, setting Josie off as well!

The county scholarship was duly taken. The children had to go to the actual school to take the exam. Josie quite enjoyed it, especially the composition (story writing) and the intelligence test, which she found quite easy. Josie was worried about that. She finished ages before anyone else and, as she had been advised, she checked the whole paper again. Some girls still hadn't finished when they were stopped and the papers collected. Now all they could do was wait.

Josie had discovered poetry writing. She found it more difficult than story writing because she had to be more concise and the actual words she used mattered more.

The BBC had just started a new children's programme called *Your Own Ideas*, in which they read out stories, poems, ideas and comments that they liked. Josie sent off several but, after the disappointment of the book, she didn't hold out much hope.

By April, Britain was doing so well that the revenge (buzz bombs) stopped and the blackout was lifted apart from at the coast.

On 6 May 1945 Germany surrendered and the war in Europe was over. Mum had been correct: 'Right' *was* on their side. Britain and her allies (friends) had won the war. Josie thought it was a pity that so many people had to die to prove it.

A day of celebration was declared. It was going to be VE Day on 8 June. Everyone was wildly, ecstatically happy. It was as though a big black cloud that had hung over Josie's childhood had drifted away!

All the mums and dads in the street got together and made a party to celebrate. All the tables they could get together were put down the centre of the street and covered with sheets and big tablecloths. Goodness knows where all the food came from, but everyone contributed. It was a real feast with red, white and blue paper hats, and flags waving.

Someone brought out a wind-up gramophone. Someone else got a team to carry out their piano for a singsong. It was the happiest day anyone could remember and Josie wanted this feeling of freedom, this wonderful, joyful day to go on for ever.

The excitement *did* go on though because, when the exam results came through, both Josie and David had gained places. The only cloud on the horizon was that Josie and the boys were to be in separate schools.

Josie got her first taste that she could remember of a banana that all the grown-ups had missed so much and raved on about. It was over-ripe and mushy and Josie hated it, though she did get to like them later on.

Then one morning when they went to the Saturday morning cinema show, there were real ice-creams on sale, choc ices and tubs, only one each allowed and they tasted like heaven.

Josie also received a letter from the BBC telling her that one of her poems was to be broadcast on Children's Hour. The whole school cheered when it was read out in Assembly. All hurried home on the day it was to be read out on *Your Own Ideas*. Fortunately everyone loved her poem, and the Head said that the local paper was going to print it. Someone unknown shouted out, 'Well done, Ginger!' and, for once, Josie didn't mind so much.

'Not bad for a ginge,' teased David.

The final piece of excitement came after school ended in the school summer holidays when Japan surrendered too. VJ Day (Victory over Japan) was declared and all of Josie's generation saw fireworks for the very first time (obtained – somehow – by Mr Sharp).

As they stood around a big bonfire, they watched the sparks fly and the colours light up all the faces of family and friends. Everyone Josie knew and loved was there. She felt as though she could burst with happiness. David nudged her. 'It's a new beginning for all of us,' he said.

It certainly is, thought Josie. A new school, new subjects, new friends and new ideas and activities, but plenty of time for old friends and family, without the worry of war taking them away. It was indeed a wonderful new beginning.

Ginger Josie had survived the war and was looking forward – along with everyone else – to the rest of her life.

Lightning Source UK Ltd.
Milton Keynes UK
UKOW04f0013250615

254090UK00001B/6/P